WHO WAS THAT !!?

A BONE CHILLING REAL LIFE HORROR STORY

P R JAYATHILAKAN

For my wife and children

for always loving and supporting me...

Contents

Preface

As I sit here, reflecting on the events that transpired in that fateful house, I'm reminded of the blurred lines between reality and the unknown. We'd always been skeptical of ghost stories, dismissing them as mere fantasy. But our experience proved that there's often truth hidden behind the whispers.

Our family's decision to rent that house seemed innocuous enough. Little did we know, it would become a descent into terror. The eerie occurrences, initially explainable by the presence of stray animals, soon escalated into something more sinister. My wife's epilepsy, triggered by fear, became a constant reminder of the malevolent force lurking in the shadows.

This story is my attempt to unravel the mystery, to shed light on the darkness that invaded our lives. It's a testament to the existence of forces beyond our understanding, forces that refuse to be dismissed. Join me on this journey into the heart of terror, where the lines between reality and the paranormal blur. And perhaps, together, we'll uncover the truth behind the haunting question: Who was that?

CHAPTER ONE

MYNA'S TRANSFER

Let me introduce myself and my family. We are from Kerala, a southern state in India, with Thrissur as our hometown. After serving for 21 years in the Indian Air Force, I joined Hindustan Aeronautics Ltd (HAL) in Bangalore, Karnataka, and retired in 2012. Since then, we have settled in Bangalore.

We are blessed with two sons and a daughter. Our daughter, Myna, is married to Manoj, a lawyer based in Thrissur. In 2008, Myna joined the State Bank of India as a clerk and was promoted to Grade-1 officer in 2017 after excelling in the internal examination conducted by the bank.

However, her promotion came with a transfer to Kallayi, in the Kozhikode district, about 110 km away. At that time, her elder son, Manu, was in the 9th grade, and her younger son, Binu, was just two years old. Myna struggled to find a trustworthy caregiver for Binu, but to no avail. She then requested us to move with her to Kallayi, as her husband couldn't leave his work. Both our sons and their wives supported Myna's request, stressing the importance of securing her job.

Eventually, we relocated to Kallayi, moving into Malabar Apartments, which was conveniently located near Kozhikode Railway Station.

Once Myna completed her probation, she was transferred to the Perumanna branch, 16 km from Kallayi. To reduce her commute, she began searching for a house closer to her new workplace.

A broker suggested an independent house on Malankali Road, Vallikkunnu, just 2 km from Perumanna.

As the broker started emphasizing the features of the house, Myna mentioned, "My parents are elderly and prefer to live near temples."

The broker responded, "Then it's a perfect fit! There are two renowned Durga temples nearby – Malankali Temple and Bhuvaneswari Temple. Both are less than half a kilometer away. In fact, the road leading to the house is named after the Malankali Temple."

Myna was impressed. "That sounds perfect for us."

The broker added, "Also, the priest of the Bhuvaneswari Temple is famous across the state for his expertise in exorcising malevolent spirits that afflicts people ! "

Surprised, Myna replied, "That's something I didn't know. We'll consider it and get back to you."

The broker nodded, "Take your time and let me know."

Later, Myna discussed the matter with some friends, who warned her about the severe water scarcity in that area during summer. When the broker followed up, Myna expressed her concerns.

The broker reassured her, "Don't believe everything you hear. Come and see the place yourself. It's better to make a decision based on what you see, not on rumors."

We felt he had a point, and agreed to visit the house.

THE RENTED HOUSE

The following Sunday, Myna and I went to visit the proposed house. After crossing Pantheerankavu town, we continued for another two kilometers until we reached Malankali Road, which began with a steep descent. At the end of this slope, we saw the broker eagerly waiting for us at the gate of that elegant house. As we stepped out of the car, he swung the gate open.

The house stood about 70-80 feet from the gate. The paved pathway was bordered by about five-foot-high areca palm plants which stood like sentries!

As we took in the beauty of the surroundings, we reached the front courtyard, paved with beautiful interlocking tiles. When we looked around, we noticed that all other courtyards too were done similarly.

The majority of the land was filled with plantain plants.

Their long, wide leaves swayed gently in the breeze. A few coconut trees and two or three young mango trees added to the lush landscape.

The property was enclosed by six-foot-high stone walls. Near the western wall, two large jackfruit trees stood tall. Adjacent to these was a newly built tin-roofed bathroom, equipped with an Indian-style toilet.

Beyond the north courtyard, the land was about 3 feet deep. A wide circular well stood in the middle of this plot.

The broker drew a bucket of water and showed it to us. The water was clear and clean. He assured us that even at the height of summer, the water level would be at least two steps deep.

Just then, the owner, Mr. Krishnan Nair, arrived on a scooter. Parking the scooter at the end of the pathway, he hurried to us and apologized, "Please excuse me for being late; there was a huge roadblock on the way."

Mr. Nair's down-to-earth attitude immediately appealed to me. Taking out the key bunch from the pocket, he opened the main door.

We began to inspect the house. The broker eagerly explained each feature as he showed us around.

The veranda had buttresses with beautifully carved wooden backrests. The car park attached to the veranda was spacious enough to park two cars.

The living room boasted a stunning display cabinet. The hall was large and divided into areas for a TV and an inverter on one end and a dining area on the other. The master bedroom had an attached bathroom-cum-toilet with neatly tiled floors and walls.

From the dining area, we entered a large storeroom fitted with numerous wall-cupboards. Next to the storeroom was the modern kitchen. Its side walls were fitted with long, shutterless windows to provide ample light and ventilation. And on the front wall, an exhaust fan was installed at a height of about 7 feet.

In addition to the earlier mentioned store, another smaller one was also found, attached to the southeast corner of the kitchen.

The door leading to the north courtyard was made of metal! And this was the only unappealing feature that we came across on the ground floor.

Next, we climbed the stairs that took us to a small square hall. From there, we accessed two large bedrooms with attached bathrooms, a study room, an open terrace at the front, and a roofed terrace at the back. The back terrace had space for a washing machine and facilities to dry clothes.

On concluding the inspection, an excited Myna asked me, "Dad, did you like it?"

I replied, "The house is spacious enough even for two families! There's a reliable well with clean water, and your office is hardly two kilometers away. What more could we need? If you agree, I'll give the owner our word."

She asked me to negotiate the rent.

Then I approached Mr. Nair and said, "The broker mentioned the rent as Rs 15,000 a month; is that negotiable?"

He replied, "Sir, Rs 15,000 per month isn't much considering the facilities provided."

At this juncture, I hesitantly expressed my concern about water scarcity during the summer months.

Mr. Nair assured that he was prepared to deepen the well if the need arose.

With this assurance, I didn't negotiate further and agreed to the mentioned rent. Finally, we paid Rs.5,000 as a token advance to secure the house.

THE NEW ENVIRONMENT

On an auspicious day, we moved into the new house surrounded by serene and tranquil scenery. The plantain plants, coconut trees, and mango trees created a peaceful ambience. The sounds of birds chirping and leaves rustling in the breeze enhanced the beauty of the scene. Baby, Binu was found to be extremely cheerful in this new environment.

My wife and I occupied the ground floor, while Myna and her family took the first floor. Manu was thrilled with his chic study room. The spacious rooms and modern amenities made our new life comfortable, and the well with crystal-clear water was a blessing as summer approached.

Myna's husband, Manoj, stayed only for two days. After settling us in, he returned to hometown promising that he would visit every Saturday and leave only on Monday morning. When he left, we felt a bit lonely, despite the pleasant surroundings.

That night, I was jolted awake around midnight by a loud noise from above. I thought Myna or Manu might have fallen from their cots. I went upstairs and checked. Both of them were found in sound-sleep. I returned to bed, suspicious. Though the noise persisted throughout the night, I didn't go *again to know the source of it.*

The next day, we shared this strange experience with our closest neighbor, Mr.Babu . He and his wife suggested, it might be a hyena that used to visit their jackfruit tree, every now and then. It might have leapt onto the tin-roof of the newly built, outside bathroom. Although the noise continued almost every night, his explanation gave us some relief. However, a question lingered in my mind: Why didn't the hyena come on the days whenever Manoj was with us!? Was it afraid of him!?

On another occasion, a strange sound emanated from the kitchen in the dead of night, resembling metal utensils clattering on the floor. Awaking my wife, we cautiously approached the kitchen. As I stepped inside, something brushed against my foot, darting onto the kitchen slab. I immediately turned on the kitchen bulb and found a large bandicoot hurrying to flee through right side window!

Determined to address this issue, I inspected the compound the following day and found a sizable hole beneath the boundary wall at the northwest corner. I promptly filled it with stones and sealed with a thick layer of grout, temporarily resolving the problem.

THE FAULTY WIRING

Later that week, I noticed something peculiar; the security light on the front-side open terrace turns on and off automatically at dusk and dawn. I asked Myna and Manu if they were responsible. They denied, claiming they weren't even aware of the switches.

As a diploma holder in Electrical Engineering, this piqued my curiosity. Could there be a light sensor inside the bulb? To test this theory, I replaced the bulb with another one nearby and observed for a week. Once again, I found only this light to be automatic!

My curiosity deepened. Upon further inspection, I discovered that this bulb could be controlled from two different locations: the upper hall and the study room.

I opened the front covers of both switchboards and found 3-inch-long brass rods inside each box, with no apparent electrical connections! It seemed as if these rods had gone unnoticed. I wondered how this could happen! No electrician would leave metal rods inside a switchboard so carelessly.

I removed the brass rods; closed the boxes and observed the light over the next few days. To my utmost surprise, there were no more automatic actions! I was baffled; how could two metal rods, without any connection to the circuit, cause the light to behave automatic?

Not long after, the house owner paid a visit. I discussed the issue with him and the very next day he sent an electrician to clear up my doubts.

After hearing the whole story the electrician said, "I have no explanation for those brass rods! But I can assure you that the automatic action you mentioned is a misunderstanding. Your daughter and grandson, unfamiliar with the switches, might have operated them in a trial-and-error manner to turn on other lights. While doing so, they probably didn't notice the security light as it's outside."

Though I agreed with his explanation I wasn't fully convinced; I had confirmed the automatic action through careful observations! Still I chose not to argue further and simply accepted his point even though the question remained unanswered in my mind...

CHAPTER FIVE

BABY'S NIGHTMARE

One midnight, Baby Binu suddenly startled awake and cried loudly without stopping. Myna tried everything to calm him down, but all her efforts were in vain. He anxiously cried and repeatedly tried to get down from the cot. No lullabies could soothe him. Finally, after exhausting himself, he slowly fell back asleep.

His nightmares became a frequent occurrence and the next day, without fail, he would develop a fever.

Binu's ongoing distress deeply saddened Manu. He discussed the issue with his friend, Shine who lived in the neighboring house to the south.

Shine revealed, "A few years ago, the teenage daughter of the previous owner committed suicide by hanging herself from that jackfruit tree." He pointed to one of the two trees standing in our compound.

Manu asked anxiously, "Oh...!?"

"Yes; People say her ghost used to trouble the family from time to time. Eventually, they decided to sell the house and move away, citing some failure in their business as the reason. That's when Mr. Krishnan Nair bought the house."

"How come!? Was he not aware of this story!? I know that his house is not far away."

"Yes, he knew; he got it very cheap!

Then Mr. Nair renovated this 20-year-old house, transforming it into this new look!"

When Manu shared this conversation with me, his voice was trembling with overwhelming fear.

I reassured him, "You shouldn't be afraid; there's no such thing as ghosts. People often create imaginary stories to instill fear in others."

Next, I enquired Mr. Babu, about the real reason behind the sale of the house.

He said, "People say many things; no one knows the real truth."

Mrs. Babu suggested to my wife, "It would be better to take him to the priest at Bhuvaneshwari Temple. He can remove any evil influences. People come from far away to be cleansed of Satan. Whoever comes, returns happy."

She added, "On Thursdays, he performs tantric pujas for this purpose. Now you don't need to take the baby to the pooja itself; just take him to the priest at your convenient time, and explain the situation. He will tell you what to do."

The next evening, I took the baby to the priest. He brought out a long black thread with a few knots in it. Closing his eyes, he recited some mantra verses and tied the thread around the baby's waist. Many people might not believe it; but from that day on, the baby was perfectly fine!

CHAPTER SIX

THE ROMANCING CATS

Days passed as usual...

Then one evening, as dusk settled in, my wife and I finished our kitchen chores. As I closed the kitchen door, a sudden cry echoed from outside, resembling that of a baby.

The sound seemed to come from our north courtyard. The cry repeated several times, so I opened the north exit door. The metal door made a loud noise, and the cry stopped abruptly.

Surveying the north courtyard, I saw nothing unusual and assumed it was the neighboring baby.

As I prepared to head back inside, the cry resumed. This time, I scanned the area more carefully.

In the fading light, I spotted two cats huddled together in the northwestern corner of the compound wall. One was a large, fat, black Tom-cat, and the other was a smaller gray Molly-cat.

Though Tom was a new guest, Molly was familiar to us. She often visited our compound, likely drawn by the scent of fish scraps. Despite their eerie cries, I hesitated to disturb them.

Returning indoors, I informed my wife: "Our Molly and her companion are on the wall, possibly waiting to mate. It's better not to disturb them now."

She exclaimed: "Why don't you get rid of them? What if the baby gets frightened!?"

Determined, I made another attempt to scare them off, but they remained unfazed. This time, I picked up a stone and threw it at them. It might have hit Molly; she ran towards the opposite corner. Tom followed her, growling furiously.

Assuming they were now far enough from the house, I returned to join my wife and enjoy time with the baby. But minutes later, the cats' cries grew louder and louder.

My wife scolded me: "I told you to chase them away! You just came back, pitying them! What about the baby? Don't you know cats crying like this at dusk could bring diseases to infants!?"

As dusk grew darker, I became more determined. I armed myself with a long stick and headed back to the scene. Upon my return, Tom growled more fiercely. Waving the stick, I startled Molly, who finally leaped down to the other side of the wall.

But Tom remained in place, growling aggressively! Just then, a stone came flying from somewhere nearby, barely missing Tom.

This only made him more furious. His eyes shone like 100-watt bulbs, and I was afraid to look at them. Before I could react, Tom suddenly darted towards me. Though shivers ran down my spine, I yelled loudly, scaring it away.

In the chaos, I stumbled and injured my left knee. Despite the pain, I felt relieved as I saw Tom running away, crossing the entrance gate.

Back inside, I shared the news with my wife, showing her my injury. To my surprise, she started laughing. I wondered what was so funny!

I showed the injury to Manu who felt sad and applied some ointment.

When Myna returned, I explained the incident. She pitied my injury, but my wife continued laughing non-stop. I felt as if she loved only the baby, not me.

Later, as we lay in bed, I turned away from her without saying a word.

To my dismay, around midnight, Binu woke up crying loudly!!

The next day, I took him back to the same priest. He removed the old thread and tied a new one around the baby's waist.

CHAPTER SEVEN

FIRST EPISODE OF EPILEPSY

Two years passed smoothly, and then, one fateful night...

Around 2 a.m., my wife got up to use the toilet. Upon returning to bed, she suddenly started screaming loudly, as if she had seen something terrifying.

I repeatedly asked, "What happened?"

But she only continued to scream...!

In the dim moonlight, the eerie shadows of swaying plantain leaves danced on the walls. I thought perhaps she had been confused and frightened by those shapes. Quickly, I turned on the light, and what I saw horrified me! Her face was sharply turned to the left, foam forming at the corners of her mouth. Her chest heaved rapidly with a harsh 'gir, gir' sound, as if she were struggling to breathe. Both her hands were clenched tightly; it was an epileptic attack.

I remembered that contact with iron could reduce the severity of epileptic symptoms. Without wasting a moment, I grabbed a bunch of keys from the cupboard and forced them into her left palm.

Within minutes, the symptoms began to subside. Her screams quieted, and the 'gir, gir' sound slowed. After a while, she attempted to speak, though with great difficulty. I guessed she was asking for water. I brought some, sprinkling a little on her face and offering her a sip. Gradually, she returned to normal and slowly fell asleep.

The next morning, around 6 a.m., our telephone rang. My younger son from Bangalore spoke in a trembling, low-spirited voice: "Sister-in-law, Soumya's father, Raghu uncle, has left us..." He paused, then continued, "At midnight, uncle went to the toilet. Back from toilet he checked on aunty who was sleeping in another room, and told her to take care of her health. He returned to his room but didn't wake up when the alarm rang in the morning. When Soumya went to wake him up, she found him unresponsive, his legs hanging off the bed."

Soumya cried out, calling for her mother who rushed in. Overcome with grief, she collapsed onto her husband's body.

The reason I connect this incident here, is this: After hearing the shocking news, my wife whispered to me in a trembling voice: "Last night, after I returned to bed from the toilet, I saw a tall man standing at the foot of the bed."

From her expression, I could see she was still gripped by fear. I tried to comfort her, dismissing it as a misunderstanding caused by shadows.

To lighten the mood, though the moment was not appropriate for jokes, I cracked one anyway: "Is it possible for a deceased person to cover such a long distance so quickly?"

CHAPTER EIGHT

NON-CEASING SEIZURES

In 2013, my wife underwent surgery to remove a tumor from her optic nerve. Afterwards, she began experiencing unexpected seizures, which would cause her to fall every time they occurred.

To prevent these seizures, she had to take a tablet called Levipill regularly; missing a dose could trigger a seizure. However, the medication seemed to cause psychological symptoms, so we switched to homeopathic remedies, hoping there would be no side effects.

Over the course of 2-3 years, her condition gradually improved, and the seizures nearly ceased.

When the epileptic episodes began to repeat, I suspected this might be a variant form of seizures. So, we again administered the same homeopathic medicines.

However, the epileptic episodes continued to plague her, occurring every 2-3 months, consistently around midnight, while she was asleep. We chose not to inform Myna and Manu, fearing it would frighten them.

One day, my wife discussed this issue with our elderly housemaid, who advised us to change rooms and place a knife under the pillow while sleeping.

Since there was only one bedroom on the ground floor, we shifted to the drawing room, rearranging the furniture to create a sleeping space. We slept on a mat with a bedsheet spread over it and placed a large knife under the pillow, determined to confront any scary or evil forces. Yet, the epileptic episodes persisted.

Once, Manu had to stay in our hometown for a week in connection with his studies. Myna then requested us to sleep in the upper hall, as she was afraid to sleep alone.

In this hall, we worshipped Lord Sree Krishna. This gave us certain comfort as we believed that his divine presence would shield us from evil forces.

However, on the fourth night, the attack recurred with full force.

Hearing my panicked voice as I tried to awaken my wife from her seizure, Myna awoke and rushed towards us.

She was terrified by the ferocious expressions on her mother's face. Despite her fear, she embraced her mother and started crying loudly. The next moment, she collapsed, unconscious, onto mother's lap.

I quickly rushed downstairs, brought a jug of water, and sprinkled it on her face. She gradually regained consciousness. By this time, her mother had also recovered from the convulsions and returned to normal.

When my wife saw Myna's state, she became deeply worried and asked what had happened to her beloved daughter. They wept together for a while, embracing each other.

Myna then turned to me and asked, "Dad, what did I just witness? How many times has mother had this problem? Why were you hiding this from me?"

At this point, I had no other choice but to explain the entire history to her.

After listening to the story, Myna was stunned for a moment before responding. Then she told, "Alright, tomorrow morning itself, we must visit the doctor."

The following morning, we consulted a homeopathic physician located merely a km from our residence. He prescribed some medicines and informed us that while the intensity of the seizures would initially decrease, it would take a minimum of 2 years for a full recovery.

Under his treatment, her health gradually improved, and the epileptic attacks became less frequent and less intense.

THE WHITE GHOST

Days passed in their usual rhythm until that fateful evening...!

The incident still terrifies me, sending shivers down my spine.

It was around 8 p.m. A light drizzle fell, accompanied by frequent thunderstorms. The windowpanes rattled in the wind, and the electricity flickered.

Everyone had finished dinner. Myna went upstairs with the baby, while I helped Manu with his math homework at the dining table.

My wife was wrapping up in the kitchen.

Suddenly, she cried out and rushed towards us, frantically gesturing at the south-facing kitchen window.

"What happened?", I asked her.

She could barely speak but pointed fearfully at the window!

She often reacted this way, even when a cockroach or beetle flew in; so, I went to check the kitchen, but nothing seemed unusual!

I tried to calm her down, "Relax; tell me what's wrong "

Through stuttering breaths she said, "something outside...!!"

"Haha...! You always get confused! It's probably just the plantain tree distorted by the lightning."

But she insisted, "No! Something's outside..., in white!"

To ease her nerves, I asked Manu to bring an umbrella and torch. We went out and searched the area but could not trace anything, extra-ordinary!

As the rain now intensified, Manu told, "Grandma must have been fooled by lightning. I am going; there is a lot to study."

We came back inside and Manu went up to his room.

As I was about to switch off the hall light, I noticed that the outside bathroom light was still on!

I told my wife, "See; the last person to use the outside toilet forgot to switch off the light; it's still on. I will turn it off and come back; you can go to bed"

I took the umbrella, but not the torch as Manu carried it back. Reopening the kitchen door, I went out again.

The wind was howling and the rain was pouring out.

While turning off the light, I noticed that the outside bolt of the door was open! I pushed the door inward; but it didn't open. At once, a chill ran down my spine as I realized that the door was bolted shut from the inside!

Just then, a branch from one of the jackfruit trees snapped and crashed onto the bathroom roof, creating a deafening noise. At the same moment, the power too went off! Overcome with fear, I dashed back to the kitchen, guided only by the lightning flashes.

Grabbing my mobile from the dining table, I called my neighbor, Babu. "Babu, please come over quickly! It's urgent!"

"What...!? Don't you know it's pouring rain and the power's out too...!? "

"Please, come fast; someone is hiding in our outside bathroom!"

"Oh...!? Is it so...!? Alright, I'm on my way, just wait!"

Babu arrived as quickly as possible, with a torch and we approached the bathroom.

Babu shouted, "whoever's inside, come out now, or you'll regret it!"

As there was no response from inside, we moved closer and Babu gave the door a hard push. To my utter surprise, it opened easily, and we didn't find anyone inside.

Babu looked at me, confused. "what's going on!? Didn't you try opening the door!?"

"Yes, I did; but it didn't open!"

For a moment, he stood silent and then said," In that case, immediately we must scan the whole compound thoroughly"

We combed through the entire area and eventually stepped onto Malankali Road, crossing the entrance gate. Babu shone the torch around and spotted, at a distance, something white moving, wavy! To me, it looked exactly like a white ghost!

I was paralyzed with fear, but Babu quickly ran over and caught the "ghost".

When came closer, I realized that it was none other than the daily wager, Mr.Kanaran who came to clean our compound whenever the house owner ordered.

"Are you out of your mind? " I shouted. "Why didn't you respond to our calls.? Don't you know that the outside toilet may be used by a worker only during working hours?"

As soon as he opened his mouth to speak out, a horrible stench hit us! It was clear that he was drunk to the point of stupor! So we left him, and decided to question the next day.

Before leaving the scene, Babu advised, "Lock the gate as soon as Myna came back from office; otherwise, you'll have unwanted visitors like this."

I went inside, changed out of my wet clothes and explained the sequence of events to my wife. Though relieved to know it was just a man, not a ghost, she still suffered another bout of epilepsy, that night too!

The next day, Mr.Kanaran came and pleaded : He had gone to buy a medicine for an upset stomach and was tricked by a friend, into drinking toddy. By the time he reached our gate, his stomach was out of control and was compelled to use our toilet. He didn't respond to our calls out of embarrassment.

He promised it wouldn't happen again.

CHAPTER TEN

WHO WAS THAT !!?

I had previously mentioned that the severity of my wife's epileptic attacks had considerably reduced under homeopathic treatment, with longer intervals between episodes. However, the attacks persisted, albeit in a milder form. Then, one night in June 2021...

As usual, we were sleeping in the guest room. It was raining heavily, and I was completely covered with a bedsheet. Around midnight, my wife woke me, saying she needed to use the toilet. She got up on her knees but remained in that position for an unusually long time. I suspected she might be experiencing a seizure.

I reached for my mobile phone, which was nearby, and tried to turn on its torch. Despite touching the torch icon many times, it wouldn't activate! Panic set in, and I frantically tried to turn it on. Finally, it lit up! What I saw at that moment — I couldn't believe my eyes! I was shocked, and my body was frozen!

In place of my wife, on her knees, was a beautiful, slim young lady in a churidar! From my position, I could see only the left side and back of the lady. She was smiling, her left-side teeth perfectly aligned and beautifully white... She had long, curly hair and looked as young as someone in her thirties...

I felt as if I were dreaming! So, I tried to regain my senses! I knew that my wife didn't have such perfectly aligned teeth or long hair, nor was she as slim as this... and she only wore sarees! Then...!? I wondered, "Who is this lady!?"

Instantly, I jumped up and turned on the room light. At that moment, what I didn't expect happened!! As soon as the room was lit, the lady disappeared, kicking my wife to the left. She fell with great force, and a loud 'tup' sound of her head hitting the wall echoed in the room!

I rushed to her and tried to lay her on her back. As usual, her frothing mouth was turned fully to the left; her chest rose and fell rapidly; her expression turned extremely ferocious...!! This state continued for one or two more minutes. Then slowly, she began to recover and tried to speak. I knew she wanted water!

I ran to the dining table, fetched a mug of water, and sprinkled some on her face. Slowly, she opened her eyes, took a sip, and within a few minutes, she regained full consciousness! It was then I noticed a cricket ball-sized lump on the right side of her scalp, close to her forehead. I wondered how the lump appeared on the right side when she fell towards her left! This remains unanswered to this day, even though the lump took nearly two months to vanish!

The very next day, I visited the priest of Bhuvaneswari temple and explained what had happened that night.

He told me, "The land where your rented house stands were once part of a burial ground! It would have been a wonder if you hadn't experienced anything before leaving this place!"

He then brought two black threads, onto which mantras were chanted. He tied one on my right wrist and wrapped the other in a small piece of paper.

Handing over the packet, he said, "Take this thread and tie it on the knuckle of her left hand. Mind you, this is only a temporary solution; to avoid more serious consequences, you must bring her next Thursday at 4 AM for the 'Tantric pooja' to remove the ghost from her body once for all.

I returned home and tied the thread to my wife's left hand. However, she refused to attend the 'Tantric pooja'.

I could have told her the truth about the land, as revealed by the priest, to persuade her to attend the special pooja. I didn't do that, as it might have brought unwarranted fear to her and other family members. Even now, it remains a secret with me.

The following month, Myna received her transfer order back to our hometown, Thrissur. And thus, we bid farewell to that ghostly house where we had stayed for more than four years. Except for the epileptic episodes, we had a peaceful stay with all the privileges given by the humble and decent owner!

Back in Thrissur, we visited an old Ayurvedic doctor. He prescribed an herbal anti-epileptic decoction. She continued it for two years and had no attacks thereafter, with God's grace! It is up to the reader to decide whether an herbal decoction could remove ghost effects!

As a final point, I must mention that one question still lingers in my mind:

"Who was that!!?"

THE END

Respected reader,

your time is precious and I'm honored you chose to spend it reading my book.

Thank you so much

About The Author

PR Jayathilakan

Author of this book PR Jayathilakan is an ex-serviceman who served in Indian Air Force for 21 Years. He brings his unique blend of his expertise and literary flair to the page. With a passion for crafting immersive and realistic stories, the author draws on his own experiences to create richly detailed worlds and complex characters. His writing is a testament to the power of storytelling to capture the human experience. This is his debut novel. Contact him at jayathilakan52@gmail.com

-By Dr. Sureshbabu Raghavan